THE PUNCTUATION STATION

In memory of
Deborah Komorn Baruch,
who loved poetry,
language, and books.

—B.P.C.

To the 3 M's
in my life, you make
me smile every day.

—J.LV.

Millbrook Press
A division of Lerner Publishing Group, Inc.
241 First Avenue North
Minneapolis, MN 55401 U.S.A.

Website address: www.lernerbooks.com

Library of Congress Cataloging-in-Publication Data

Cleary, Brian P., 1959—
    The punctuation station / by Brian P. Cleary : illustrations by Joanne Lew-Vriethoff.
        p.   cm.
    ISBN: 978–0–8225–7852–9 (lib. bdg. : alk. paper)
    1. English language—Punctuation—Juvenile literature. I. Lew-Vriethoff, Joanne, ill. II. Title.
PE1450.C545 2010
428.2—dc22   2009015860

Manufactured in the United States of America
1 – VI – 12/15/2009

THE PUNCTUATION STATION

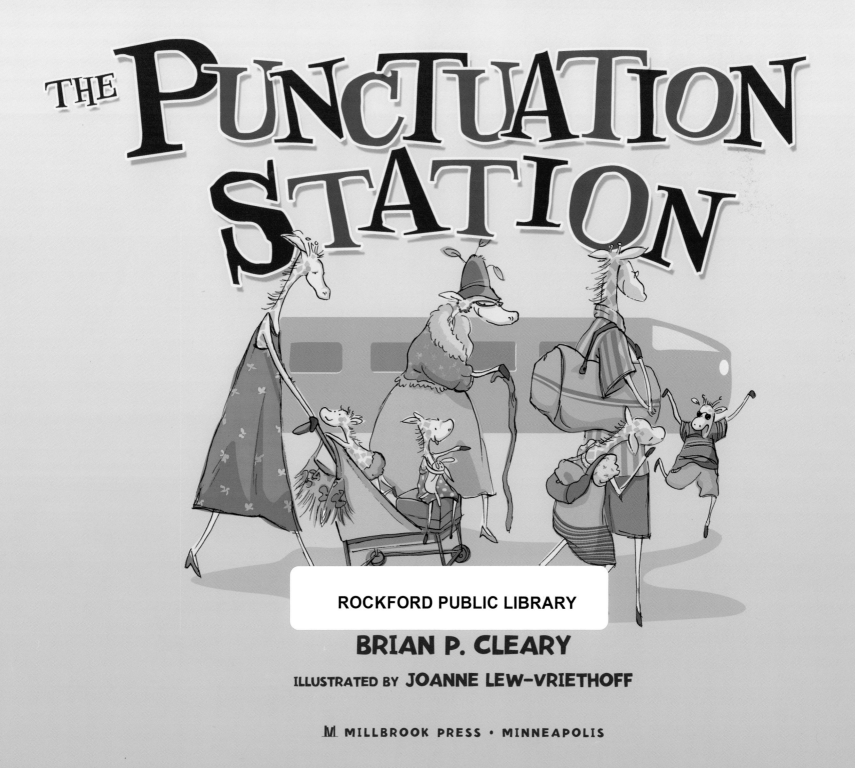

BRIAN P. CLEARY

ILLUSTRATED BY **JOANNE LEW-VRIETHOFF**

M MILLBROOK PRESS · MINNEAPOLIS

Punctuation comes in marks—
some straight, some round, some curly.
And once you get to know them,
you can punctuate quite surely.

This is called a period.
You put it at the end
of each abbreviation or each
sentence that you've penned.

TICKETS

Hi,
Mom.

Dr. Mayday

Taxis,
Limos,
etc.

Ask us
about our
limo
service.

?

TRACK 3
TRACK 4 →

TRACK 1
TRACK 2 →

PAUSE
FOR
AN ICE
CREAM
COMMA

EXCLAMATION
POINT
IS FUN

train stops

train stops

Ms. Ozz

13

ASKOff MOO'S
Ice Cream, Candy, & Treats

The comma is a curly mark.
It makes us pause a bit
before a word or phrase, you see.
You separate with it.

, COMMA

15

Also, when you're making lists,
the comma can be used
to keep apart the items
so the reader's not confused.

STATION RULES

NO bare feet, running, yelling, spitting, littering

YES walking, indoor voices, polite behavior

Thank you.

When making a contraction, you'll use this—apostrophe—and put it where the letters you're replacing used to be.

, APOSTROPHE

19

It's also very useful when
you're saying who owns what,

like Caitlin's kite

and Josh's light

and teacher's
great big mutt.

CHECK BAGS HERE

21

These are called quotation marks.
You've seen them when you've read.
They go before and just behind
the words that someone's said.

They also come in handy when we find ourselves repeating something quite exact that we have taken from our reading.

THE BEGINNER'S GUIDE TO TRAIN TRAVEL

BY Ima N. Ginear

"Taking a train is a fine way to travel from one place to another."

from The Beginner's Guide to Train Travel

The question mark looks like
an ear above a dot of ink.
This bit of punctuation's
quite important, don't you think?

Hyphens are those little lines
that link together words
or parts of them, as in
Great-grandma's ex-friend got two-thirds.

EXCLAMATION POINT

Here's a sign that's just a line
with one small dot below it—
use it when you're shocked or pumped
and not afraid to show it!

33

So now when someone asks you
if you know your punctuation,
you can answer "yes!"
with an excited exclamation!

We're here!

PUNCTUATION STATION

PUNCTUATION

PERIOD •

A period comes at the end of a sentence. It also follows some abbreviations.

EXAMPLE: Dr. Brown is riding the train.

COMMA ,

A comma tells you where to pause when reading a sentence. It also separates items in a list.

EXAMPLE: On the train, the girl met a bear, a chicken, and a cat.

APOSTROPHE '

An apostrophe takes the place of one or more letters in a contraction. It also shows ownership.

EXAMPLE: This is Brian's seat. It isn't mine.

QUOTATION MARKS " "

A set of quotation marks tells you when someone is talking. If you are copying something someone else wrote, you also put it in quotation marks. Comic books don't use quotation marks. Instead, they put a character's words in a word balloon.

EXAMPLE: "I'm reading about railroads," said Joanne.

INFORMATION

QUESTION MARK ?

A question mark comes at the end of a question.

EXAMPLE: When will the train arrive?

HYPHEN —

A hyphen joins words in a compound adjective that comes before a noun.
(A compound adjective is two or more words that make a single adjective.)
A hyphen is also used when spelling out fractions and the numbers 21 to 99.

EXAMPLE: The well-known author wrote twenty-one books about trains.

EXCLAMATION POINT !

An exclamation point comes at the end of a sentence that expresses excitement, anger, or another strong feeling.

EXAMPLE: I can't wait to read this book again!